# Iris and Walter
# True Friends

# Iris and Walter
# True Friends

WRITTEN BY

Elissa Haden Guest

ILLUSTRATED BY

Christine Davenier

GULLIVER BOOKS

HARCOURT, INC.

SAN DIEGO   NEW YORK   LONDON

For Cherry the great, with all my love    —E. H. G

For Sylvie Ferron    —C. D.

www.harcourt.com

First Gulliver Books paperback edition 2002
*Gulliver Books* is a trademark of Harcourt, Inc., registered
in the United States of America and/or other jurisdictions.

Library of Congress Cataloging-in-Publication Data
Guest, Elissa Haden.
Iris and Walter true friends/written by Elissa Haden Guest;
illustrated by Christine Davenier.
p.  cm.
"Gulliver Books."
Summary: Walter shows Iris how to make friends with
his horse Rain, and in turn, Iris helps Walter deal with a
problem at school.
[1. Horses—Fiction. 2. Schools—Fiction. 3. Friendship—
Fiction.]  I. Davenier, Christine, ill.  II. Title.
PZ7.G9375It  2001
[Fic]—dc21    00-8211
ISBN 0-15-202121-3
ISBN 0-15-216448-0 (pb)

I  H  G  F  E  D  C  B
H  G  F  E  D  C  B  A  (pb)

PRINTED IN SINGAPORE

# Contents

6

# 1. Dreaming of Rain

Iris dreamed of riding Rain
over green meadows,
down a path of pines,
straight into the sparkling stream.

"You can't ride Rain,"
said Walter.
"Why not?" asked Iris.
"Because," said Walter,
"Rain is fast and wild."
But Iris *wanted* to
ride Rain.

The next day, Iris put on her cowgirl boots.
She put on her cowgirl hat.
Then she and Walter went to see Rain.

"Yoo-hoo, Rain. Come here!" shouted Iris.
But Rain only snorted and stamped her hoof,
then galloped away.

"Why doesn't she come?" asked Iris.
"Because," said Walter, "horses don't
like shouting."
"Oh," said Iris.

The next day, Iris brought Rain a present.
"Come here, Rain," said Iris.
"I brought you Grandpa's special cookies."
But Rain did not come.

"Why doesn't she come?" asked Iris.
"Because," said Walter, "horses can be shy."
"Walter, what do horses like?" asked Iris.
"Horses like clucking and carrots and
gentle hands," said Walter.
"Hmm," said Iris.

# 2. Riding Rain

The next day, Iris and Walter
went to see Rain.
They had carrots. They had hope.
They had a plan.
Iris held out a carrot.
"Come here, Rain," she said.
But Rain did not come.

"Why doesn't she come?" asked Iris.
"Try clucking," said Walter.
So Iris clucked and clucked.
Rain moved backwards.
Rain moved sideways.
But still, Rain did not come.

"Maybe Rain doesn't like me," said Iris.
"Maybe Rain is scared of you," said Walter.
"Don't be scared of me, Rain," said Iris.

Every day, Iris and Walter went to see Rain.
Every day, Iris clucked and clucked—
and held out a carrot.

Then one day, Rain walked slowly, slowly
over to Iris.
Iris felt Rain's hot breath on her hand.
Rain stared at Iris. Then *chomp*—
she ate the carrot!
"Oh," said Iris.

Day after day, Iris and Walter
went to see Rain.
They fed her carrots.
They stroked her neck.

They sang sweet
songs in her ear.

Then one fine day, Iris climbed
up on Rain's back.

"Hold on, Iris. Hold on tight," said Walter
"Whatever you do, don't let go!"

And then Rain took off!
Away Iris rode, over green meadows,
down a path of pines,
straight into the sparkling stream.

"Oh, Walter! Did you
see me? Did you see me
riding Rain?" asked Iris.
"Yes, you are very brave,
Iris." said Walter.
"Thank you, Walter,"
said Iris.
"May I have a turn
now?" asked Walter.
"You bet!" said Iris.

# 3. The First Day of School

It was the first day of school.
Iris was scared.
"I don't want to go to school,"
Iris told her mother.
"I know, my Iris,"
said Iris's mother.
"I don't want to go to school,"
Iris told her father.
"I understand, my Iris,"
said Iris's father.

"Do I have to go to school?"
Iris asked Grandpa.
"Yes, my girl," he said.
"And when you come home,
you will have my special
cookies."

So Iris walked slowly, slowly
up the steps with Walter.
"I feel cold and scared," Iris said to Walter.
"Iris, you are very brave," said Walter.
"I *know* you are brave enough to go to school."
But Iris did not feel brave.

"Good morning," said Miss Cherry.
Miss Cherry took Iris's cold hand
in her own warm hand.

"Come right on in," she said, smiling.
"Welcome to school."

"Hey, Walter," whispered Iris,
"I think school is fun."
"Me, too," said Walter.
"And Miss Cherry is great," said Iris.
"The greatest," said Walter.
But that afternoon, something happened.

At snack time, Miss Cherry said,
"Today it will be Walt's turn to
pass out the cookies."
Walter did not know
what to do.
He did not like to be
called Walt.

"Don't forget me, Walt," said Benny.
"Over here, Walt!" called Lulu.
*This is terrible*, thought Walter.

On the way home from school,
Walter said, "Iris, I don't want
Miss Cherry to call me Walt."
"Why don't you tell her?" asked Iris.
"I just can't," said Walter.
That night, Walter had a hard time
going to sleep.

# 4. The Second Day of School

The next morning,
Walter woke up early.
He wrote out the letters
        W-A-L-T.
But they didn't look right.

Suddenly something white
floated in his open window.
It was a paper airplane!
Walter unfolded the airplane.

There was a note.

Iris had drawn a picture of herself.
She had written her name in big letters.

Walter smiled.

"Iris, Iris!" he shouted.

"Out here, Walter!" she called.

"You gave me an idea," said Walter.

"I'm so glad," said Iris.

"There's something I have to do," said Walter.

"I'll meet you at school."

All during music,
Walter thought about
his idea.
He was worried.
What if it didn't
work?

Finally, it was time for show-and-tell.
Benny showed his puppet.
Lulu did a magic trick.

At last, it was Walter's turn.
Walter showed everyone
his painting.
"This is me," he said.
"Walter—W-A-L-T-E-R."

Miss Cherry looked at Walter's painting. Then she looked at Walter and smiled. "Why, that is a wonderful painting, *Walter*," said Miss Cherry.

When the last bell rang,
Miss Cherry said,
"Good-bye, Iris. Good-bye, Walter."
"See you tomorrow, Miss Cherry,"
they said.

Outside, Grandpa was waiting.
"So how was the second day of school?"
he asked.
"It was wonderful!" said Iris and Walter
together.

The illustrations in this book were created in pen and ink on keacolor paper.
The display type was set in Elroy.
The text type was set in Fairfield Medium.
Printed and bound by Tien Wah Press, Singapore
Production supervision by Sandra Grebenar and Wendi Taylor
Designed by Lydia D'moch